Electric Blue Heaven

Thanks Sara, :)
I hope you enjoy the poems!

Electric Blue Heaven

Benjamin James Mclay

ELECTRIC BLUE HEAVEN. Copyright © 2021 by Benjamin James Mclay. All rights reserved. No part of this book may be used or reproduced in any manner whatsoever without written permission except in the case of brief quotations embodied in critical articles and reviews.

ISBN: 978-0-6452702-0-4 (PAPER EDITION)
ISBN: 978-0-6452702-1-1 (HARDCOVER)
ISBN: 978-0-6452702-2-8 (EPUB)

for Kimberley

Table of Contents

City Walking

electric blue heaven 15
life is a beautiful suffering 17
metropolis 19
single origin 20
fancy dress 22
metres apart 24
heaven is the place you reside 25
a fetish for the lost parade 27
I took a drive down the coast 29
australian summer 30
meteor shower 32

Something Chemical

there is always something with someone 37
at the zoo 39
a pink pounding 40
slow dancing 42
kitchen disco 43
lover 45
for kimberley 47
stupid poem 49
something chemical 50
moping 53
the risk 55
farewell 56
jamie 57

Amongst the Death Adder Sleep

joy machine 61
laniakea 62
pilgrimage 64
pissing contest 65
scarlett 68
it doesn't always come when you call 70

oxford street 71
never alone 74

Salt in the Wounds Opens the Heart Eyes

trick of the light.. 79
take out on the couch 80
we can only record the times 82
the lake... 85
worm food.. 87
cherchez la femme 89
infirmity 91
portals... 93
to the people in horror row... 94
black tobacco 95

Like Incense Burning Away

magnum opus... 99
what's the matter, benny? 100
don't shoo away the butterfly 103
hungry hippos... 104
eels in the creek.. 105
venus lake... 106
we are old... 108
freak show.. 110
the longest days must have end.. 113

The Comings and Goings of Night Trains

never mind the name of it 117
in the forest 119
tango... 120
equals 121
sad anime 123
poet... 124
unfortunately.. 128
feathers on the wind 129
out of our control 130

Urban Birds

ignorance isn't bliss 135
tips and tricks 137
bushfires 140
death to a parisian cliché 142
good friday 143
masters and meal tickets 146
pemberton party 148

The Tugging Shapes of Sky

images that last 153
orion's belt 155
fractals 156
kintsugi 159
supernatural cathedral woman 161
art is quite useless 163

Door Knocking

chastity belt 169
membership revoked 171
follow the heart and you'll never go wrong 174
maestro 175
nightfall 177
dancing in the dirt 178
witch hunts 180
reach 182

Russian Caravan

machines in the garden 187
fear no endings 189
eyes of the undine 191
portugal 192
call the muses home 194
contender 195

take me on a joy ride 197
consider this a sign 199
amphoras 202

In Hindsight

fervour 205
blood pacts 207
laya 208
heartbreak 210
the films are wrong 211
god is a woman 212
on days apart 213
we left the garden 214
hallstatt 216

I

City Walking

electric blue heaven

there is an efficacious beauty
in the demise of all things;
a heaven in the resignation of self.

we begin
with some heat,
some burn—
electric and blue;
anguish for the voyage,
and then it breaks

to run wild
into flesh
and ruin
and echo along the wandering
as we become phantoms
to those
we leave behind.

though, we must know
the answer to our own sum
beyond
and tear rest down like a pillar
and scrape knuckle
to catch to the circles end
and drown
as form undone
reveals
the rain is real;
it smothers us all
ever since the gloomy wood abandoned…

no more shade
to the fabled
and the winged,
and some afternoons

I go down to the water
and the snakes and their atoms
fold back into the sun
whilst the soul
dies on the horizon.

and on days like this,
nothing matters—
not the spell
or doors closed
or pain in the gut,
just the absence of the veil
because that's how we all go in the end:
unanswered
like fire doused by rain
washed over
like some temporary thing…

life is a beautiful suffering

all
pile
into
the great comedy.
the horn is blaring
and the kids are alright;
they are giving it away
to cameras, convertibles,
implants, nightclubs,
churches and mosques,
blasphemy and teardrops,
sunflowers and radiation
with robins on their backs.

roll your own cigarettes.
brown bottles
in brown bags,
fire-breathing managers,
plastic cards
        and bank accounts
emptied on sail trips
to monolithic blocks
on islands far, far away.
they are all here:
those high on faith,
those poor in fetish—
all welcome escape
in suits, in aprons, in gyms
in beds, in hospitals,
cafes, art galleries—
spending themselves
in the perpetual war
foot
        to
                floor
        on the pedal.

what's it all for?
I don't know…
ask the fog outside my door,
ask the sheep in glass towers,
ask the places with stains
that won't go away,
ask the ones who leave quickly,
ask the ones who stay long,
ask the animals behind bars
and the actors
with clipped wings
trying to stay relevant.

they will all tell you
it's alright,
it's not that bad;
there are things left to bargain for:
seven billion morons
and me,
kicking it to some false sense of urgency.

why do we endure?
because there is no tragedy here
just comedy
man
is the animal
that laughs at himself.

metropolis

in the spine
of a place so young,
the people are the city.

otherwise, it would be
empty grey towers
and streets
with names
that don't mean anything
to anybody…

single origin

bountiful
beans!
I have
masturbated
three
and a half
times today
and
have written
three
and a half poems.

whatever
was in
that morning cup
could've given
a pulse
to Ramesses the third.

dark magic,
junkie fever;
it has travelled, no doubt.
black
and bitter—
somewhere from the likes
of Vista al Bosque.

and there,
a farmer rises
next to a warm
Latin American ass.

he washes his face,
tends to his field,
smokes a dark chocolate cigarette
in a crumbling sun hat

unaware
that he
is a
poet...

fancy dress

sitting
in
the
corner
of
a
hotel
room
in my two-dollar suit
and staring at a painting on the wall
inside a sunray,
a small ship
evades dark clouds.

I walk out
onto the balcony,
light a cigarette
with a match
and look down,
way below
at all the suckers
crawling like insects
under the shadow of God.

I think of the storm—

not now,
not for me.

I walk inside
grab the thigh of blondie
sitting on the edge of the bed,
drawing on thick black smoky eyes,
breasts out,
plate of chips at her side,
cackling at a soap opera.

she gets up
and lays one on me.
I zip her into a fancy number.

"where shall we go?" she asks.

"you look deadly accurate," I say
and
fiddle
with the soft bits.

she slaps me and smiles.

I think of
the small rays
of light...

metres apart

most of us
walk between
the borders of temporal joy
and unyielding despair.

and though we walk alone,
we are *not* alone.

behind the give-way,
the blood-donning,
the holding of elevators,
we live like tiny allies—

and in the next room,
in the passing cars,
behind these words,
you
and
I
at
an
arm's
length.

and for a moment
we share
like strangers;
lost and found
in each other,
ignoring
the great divide.

heaven is the place you reside

today
has had a slow death
and asked for colours
in its mourning.
I am two beers down
and the birds
above this fast car fly
whilst the world
falls away
in lines—
cool
blue
waters
are waiting for us.
how long
can we be this young?
I grab your leg,
you smile at me;
       it becomes all you:
hair
and light,
body and sundress
like something supernatural,
blowing in the wind—
and as we pull up,
you take off
down to the water;
a shadow
dancing
in the eye of the sun.
and there you are:
a pearl
on the beach
spinning atop the sand—
and you don't
have a care

in the world…

a fetish for the lost parade

on a park bench;
it doesn't take long.

in bars
or cafes;
it doesn't take long.

in the factory,
hospital
or brief red-light stall;
it happens even sooner.

in this crowded solitude,
a silent exchange;
I am bewitched by ordinary beings.

an imprint
so heavy,
drunken revelry occurs.
and in these moments,
I adopt their madness,
their saintlike desperation,
their precious hopings,
their murdersome kinks.

without consent,
they bare their nakedness before me.
and in infinity museums,
I rewrite their stories
and experience us together
entwined in cosmic duality.

oh, the horror!

the pleasure

the perversion

the sad animation imagined here.

it is like this I see you,
know you,
feel your truth.

and the terrible thing is:
most people don't have the guts to be themselves.

but I wait and wait
and watch
for momentary surrenders
when echoes leak out…

because you all have something—
every single one of you.
it is there on the corner of your mouth,
in the way tears form on your eye,
in the way you move your hands.
playful in the wind,
in the passenger seat of a car.
you all have something:
an honest movement,
a unique chord—
and when I hear them play,
I am reminded of my own:

that human silence,
that human sound.

I took a drive down the coast

two hundred grand
for a hunk of metal
and seagulls still shit on the bonnet.

"nice car"
I shout across the lane being polite;
got to give the man his envy.
he laughs and inflates;
the man is his own champion.

could've been me:
white collar thrills
if I was not haunted
by the wild blue yonder.

I suppose we all trade our time for something…

and after the green,
we drive alongside a little more,
and my paint-stripped horse
(which refuses the bed of retirement)
still gets me the same distance.
I still feel the wind,
      see the birds
        and sky as *he*.

I wonder if losing your hair
in a Ferrari is all that different
or if fearing god on the backseat of the bus
still feels the same…
I wonder what it would be like
to look down at the ants
from those brown leather seats
and feel pride from a Sunday ride
to love something
that has no soul.

australian summer

the air conditioning doesn't work.
there are parasites in my tea
like mosquitoes in a duck pond;
brown bitter shit
blending five hundred
white sheets of paper
into considerable nonsense.

this gig requires honesty,
and I am not the truest thing.
I fall rapidly to the devil
and find the road to redemption
ever so boring.

beyond me
lies something good:
dandelion nipples
and gooseberry charm,
cars camped on the curbside,
flooding the white-hot sand
with the beautiful
and the bold
oiling themselves up like sausages,
a lucrative summer tease
selling postcards
and aloe vera regrets.

I could join them;
I could walk out there,
but there is a bell ringing all the time
in the ears of the stubborn.
guilt would rob me of the joy.

alas resistance!
the great evil,
the invisible enemy.

it just won't do
when there is pain in the heart
and it must come out to no applause.

and the hardest part is sitting down…

and if you are
also cursed with the bells,
you will know what it is like
to ask your own reflection
      why is it so hard
           to bleed in front of each other.

meteor shower

pull
down
the fires
of heaven.

crush
this
little
town

so that
the guts
stain
the gravel

and
the bricks
and
the police cars
and
the fast food signs
become
the bedrock
in
the sea floor
again.

last time,
they passed above:
the eagle was in power,
Australia was just a word
and wilderness held the majority.

last time,
they came;
there were no

cut-and-paste homes,
minivans and station wagons,
plastic green bins
and birds
making nests
in cell towers.

and they weren't late…
the reporter promised eight;
it is eight forty-five.

I light a cigarette
and dangle my feet
from the water tower.

then
they
begin…

It is quiet;
I have nothing more to say.

I think of her
sleeping
somewhere
in the impact zone

and raise
my middle finger
to the hot
secret codes
disappearing above me,
impossible to catch

like
blonde

streaks
of memory
zooming past
in
the black.

II

Something Chemical

**there is always something with someone
somewhere
left unfinished**

dust ache,
spire,
great Spaniard emerged
to challenge,
wipe away
this immortal brim.

shade underneath
against shadow afar
and my eyes carry me
to the end of forms.

on the walls,
the abyss is broken
by halos
humming in the night.

here in circles
around the streetlamps,
I am aware of you—
and though I am a travelling man,
you are there in these halos
ahead and behind.

I have said your name softly
to them,
to no one,
to the midnight tones,
the empty streets
and empty cars,
to the open windows
and bars abandoned.

and the factory turbines

tunnels
          planes
                    taxi exhaust
know the wind
who knows the blueprint
of my spirit.

and the hills,
the runways,
roads and trees,
have heard a secondary tale.

when you walk by
do they whisper to you?

some nights,
under halos like these,
I hear my name
called from the sidewalk,
and I wonder if it is you
who has whispered to me…

at the zoo

they
are
all
together:

lions
on the sun rock

playful otters with their offspring

chimpanzees
picking at their ticks.

they
examine
us
through
the bars;
we carry
and consider
our apartness.

and by
the polishing
of our civilised cages,
we have lost
the platonic
agenda.

and so
we are all
touch-starved…

a pink pounding

between
the
arcs
of
a
four
poster
bed,

the spirits
dance
wildly in us.

they rock
and batter
the freshly-painted walls.

they shake violently
like a fever
trying
to evaporate
the maze.

eyes open,
eyes closed…
it doesn't matter.

moaning
and melting
and accelerating into liquid heat.

the brain spasms,
the muscles explode,
the chorus dies.

there is not a quarrel

with misery
or job-hunting
or thoughts of the grave.

the searching stops.

nothing
feels
so
alive.

you can be alone
or alone together.

there are many ways
to forget the body.

many ways!

and the spirits
are always itching
to escape.

and if we are lucky,
if the writing,
the painting,
the music
or the fucking
is
good enough,

we can
surpass
the vessel.

slow dancing

the
bodies
are
starving.

and in
separate rooms,
pearlescent
thoughts
of desire
go cold

to the late-night
lingering
outside bedroom doors.

almost a knock,
almost the word,
almost the touch,
almost the pleasure sounds…

how
much
of our loving
has died
to
almosts?

kitchen disco

silver threads
in a boiling
      muddy
           womb.

here, the bodies conspire—

and I am scared of burning you alive,
whereas you are scared of not adding enough fuel.

nearby,
pretty young bullets
delete
into
a handsome hell

and the cigarette butts
on tiles underfoot
crunch like cellophane;
everyone is drinking carton wine.

tied over the light bulb,
a red grocery bag
pretends
to be a sun.

the silence between us
all means nothing.
we are all bottled up:
sweaty midnight shapes
wrapped in paper applause.
useless
because we all burn
in this dark red room.

there is nothing else known.

miles away inside, we spin within
the hour promised to the flesh,
dark continents
wanting to be swept away
to where
        desire and torment
                      transcend.
I understand now—
why Adam and Eve
shacked up
and did the wild thing:
because looking at each other wasn't enough…

lover

what
lies
in the deep
groves of your husk?

the unseen world:

the cave paintings
that record your history
drawn by the inner child
on your anatomic walls.

I want to explore
those folds
under breasts,
legs
and hips,
and understand with touch
their mathematical victory;

to slide
and rise in the wet fury
and taste
the brain,
the poems,
your earthly noise;

to be inside of you
in the many ways:

the carbon,
the marrow,
the blush—

to be inside of you

and in the very same breath,
science those eyes
that reach
like vines
into the lost spaces
in me;

to know you
once,
twice,
more
and more
and more…

until
exhausted,
we
lay
draped over
each other
like
trembling webs
of
light.

for kimberley

sweet fire and
midnight copper
beneath the lamp.
crumbs in the bed.
one foot in a sock,
the other lost over the side.
pillow anthems
hang around.
yellow and hazy
from some place we were before.

it is grand to be used
for such violent purpose.
sweet fire,
the best seed for strangers.
there is religion in it;
the same as the trees.
I suppose I am an advocate—
a preacher perhaps.
we, who are meant to be shared.

and in my mind,
I will carry this
as Tristan carried Isolde.

precious
golden
lover.

antidote
to a multitude
of banal scenes.

we must survive this place
engulfed
in warm swells

of
sweet fire.

I have found more God
in bed with you
than I have ever found between
church walls and temple halls.

stupid poem

roses
are
red,

violets
are
blue.

I'm going
to bed.

you
should
come
too…

something chemical

if there is life out there
half as perverted
and they look back
through long brass telescopes,
they will see:

my bookshop angel,
the dark wood,
oil paint stains on the floor,

ugly figures,
shapes of distress—
all under a sixty-watt bulb

hands
between a blue skirt
playing the violin
rubbing back and forth
            back and forth
until the soft
cotton panties
soak through—

wetter than the oceans,
where the first cells split:
    the slime in the crucible,
    the tetra pods mounting on dry land,
    the cave-dwellers
        stripping the berries
            to campfire;

stronger
than the pull of Helen and Paris
and the thrusts that sacked Troy;

more agony

and excitement
than Schiele's forms
or the sixties heartthrobs
in maximum bloom—

centuries engrossed,
something chemical.
the pulsating
red
fury of flesh,
its magnetic design.
the liquid
warmth
between cordial
temples
is much better
than the alternative.

if there is life out there,
however unlikely,
let us hope
when they find us—
if they do—
our laughing
and our nakedness
will be dust in their eyes.

and if there were anything
left of us
comforting
any image
entertaining
in the black-sky cinema…

it would be made
from the silhouettes

of bodies
in the heat
of love-making.

moping

what happened to my girl?
she was there in the doorway…
eggs,
greens,
rice
and mushrooms on the frypan.

holy, holy morn!
everlasting
dried flower
in a brown beer bottle.

I sit alone
but not lonely
in her studio
as the people in her paintings roll their eyes;
I deserve every inch of their pity.
I am
not
immortal like them.
I have so few days…

did she go out for bread?
where did the sun go?

it would take
a thousand winning horses set free
and a king's ransom to lift my mood
or just
one
woman…

what happened to my girl?

take her
and you might as well draw the curtains

and throw the whole damned world
in the trash.

the risk
(we can love them, and they may never come back)

who waits upon that cliff
above the raging sea
fighting cold in their longing
and stares unflinching and unencumbered
by distance in-between?

who waits upon the lonely isle
amongst the soaring playful wind—
ghost of true touch,
bully to skin's feverish yearn—
and instead hears the voice of promise renewed?

who marches the lengths of the sundown sands,
remembering arms and heart beside,
cradling the fire of hopes return
on sight of the remissive tides?

who waits upon that cliff,
looking out to the nowhere sky
for love,
for you,
for *home*?

farewell

what
can
we
do
now?

the room,
the bonds,
the eyes—
all are barren.

do you remember
the music
that we make
no more?

unfortunately
hiding
a
wound
doesn't stop
its
bleeding…

and like Babylon
and its erased tapes,

we cannot
recover
what
is
lost.

jamie

my memories are moth eaten.

so from within my D.N.A chamber,
I borrow your phantom
from time.

ordinary
objects
tainted
with
the
echoes
of a life.

book spines
of the deepest green.

white toy cars.

my father,
his brothers,
the borrowed comedy,
laughter burnt into film.

not much,
just a handful…

the leftover
colour rays
assemble
a hologram,

and though
the image
may be static
with room

for false transmission.

when I thought of you
in the hills of Scotland
and amongst the trees
at Waimana bay,

a presence
lifted the dark shroud
and I was no longer
so terrified
of solitude.

III

Amongst the Death Adder Sleep

joy machine

happiness isn't rare;
it's found in a drug store,
in a cheap bottle of malt
in isle fourteen
bay twelve.

happiness is a gimmick
on daytime tv,
a secret affair,
an advert,
a news story;
the same one they always play.

happiness is a single cigarette
burning slowly from its draw.
it's the popcorn behind the sofa,
a bottle of lube,
a monthly subscription,
a replica painting from a galleria.

it's a new toaster,
a broken fridge,
a carton of milk,
a dying plant,
an old shirt,
another bill.

don't kid yourself;
it's an expensive life,
a happy one,
and the price is paid with pain.

laniakea

pickled radish,
kicking stones,
bees doing
their holy work
on the sidewalk.

old men
casting bread crumbs
on a lake.

spells of matter
suspended between floating glass
like some lost atoms
in the graveyard of stars.

insects on reeds
picked at by black wings,
algae bloom on the water.

and in my hands,
the mighty oak,
now a pencil.

where are the words,
fractures of gold
in a mountain side?

and in every passing day,
in every passing eye,
a thousand highways
lead
to
extraordinary
nowhere.

so much is lost,

too much discarded.

but it is the way of things;
plenty enough remains.

and by the passing clouds,
light strings gather
on the ground

and the trees
speak in movements:
do not clutch at shadows
and lose the sun...

pilgrimage

in the tangling
of the soul-pit,
on the march
to the inner well,

do we walk
to our despair?

do we walk
to our illumination?

pissing contest

I watch quietly,
the maddening of stone,
as two middle-aged ogres
mumble and piss in the basin sink.

they blame
the government,
their wives,
their jobs,
for the catastrophe of their lives.

and all along,
the western stage
pubs have been crowded
with more desperate ballads,
choirs of men,
cretins alike—
too weak to conquer something.

the weekend
is always alive
with their exorcisms.

I wandered in here
to drain the lizard
and witness the slow death
of the living.

my turn:
batter up!

my pepper starts to stream.
I eye the ruins on the cave walls:
graffiti and bird shit
mixed together
into a low-budget Pollock.

in my opinion,
crop circles are the most
underground art.

there are too many cocks
and not enough balls.

and now, they stuff the void
between the legs
with bravado
and resuscitate high-school triumphs
and sing chants from sport teams
and dry-hump posters of V8 cars,
trying to resurrect their old haunts
before the babes
and extra hours
and hooks,
hooks,
hooks,
dragging them—
so barely recognizable—
to the bottom
of suburban bay.

it is difficult to watch
the castration
of the masses
when Virgil waits
at the edge of the bathroom
with the door wide open.

unfulfilled potential
remains the greatest sin.

it is never too late.
it is

never
too late…

but don't expect
wisdom,
good choice,
aim
or illumination
from
any man
with his dick
in his hands.

scarlett

praise the heavens,
the infinite atom,
for pulling
the stellar strings.

it is autumn;
there are no leaves.

I am
bare
as a pagan
on the white sheets
reading Miller.

Scarlett,
done with soaping her hair,
slips out of the bath.

bless Lilith!
the golden bottom,
the sacrificial rib.

the nudity
reminds me
of
Eden…

under
the heat lamp,
the forest
is burning—

looking at her,
leaning against the mirror
like some sticky wet dream…

oh,
daughter of Eve—
find me not
in thoughts of Adam
or in the grace
of your ruling God.

I wish only
to be the apple,
the one you want
when the world
says no.

it doesn't always come when you call

thirty-one roses
stuck to my roof
with swords in-between,
and a light hangs itself
cold like an anvil of ice.

I have pulled it down
to crush my skull;
it has exposed nothing.
I have offered it beer
and cigarettes—
and still,
it does not sing.

so, I sit
in the room
like a flag with no wind
because tonight
is not a night for writing;
it is a night
for sucking teeth
and pulling hair
and pouring cider down the sink.

sometimes
you have to let it go
like an ex-lover
or be swallowed
by the sea of waiting.
it's a hard thing
to let something die
after it is already dead.

oxford street

in the east
they kill children
by the bomb.
in the west
they kill children
in the schools
with gunfire
and police brutality.
there is a disease
somewhere in Asia
that is getting them too.

and I sit here
at this corner café
amongst the binary violence,
amongst the hellfire
and cake
and the fat women laugh at each other
whilst their husbands' ears bleed.

their solemn faces want sport
and I want peace,
but the tv noise
is too low to drown them out.
the sunlight outside.
too confronting.
so, I stay.

the morning has failed us all.
I came here
to smoke, drink coffee
and drive the fox from the burrow.
instead,
I threw the remote in the bin
and ventured into a daydream,
a journey into earth's last wild.

although,
nothing good surfaced
except guilt.

how many
more deserving
can no longer
stare at the wall,
at the street,
at the sky
and dream
of punching the sun,
of voices,
faces,
designs that hurt?

no more peripheral joys
and temporary pleasures.
no more dawns
or teeth in apples
or roads that lead to
nowhere,
somewhere,
home.

nothing left to the coffin fire—
nothing at all.

and despite the coy smile
from a pretty girl
in a moving car,
I still feel the same.
the silence,
it never leaves;
it follows wherever I go.

sometimes, it's loud—
louder than any bomb or gun.
sometimes, it's as agreeable as sin.
it is heavy—
the war—
and I am heavy.
yet, some small incessant thing
endures
for some reason…

I cannot bend the knee.
this is the only war that matters:
the one for silent children
and stories screaming within.
I can hear them,
I can hear mine,
and their voices
bend the light inside
and urge me to carry on.

never alone

bejewelled seas
beauty and terror
      the rivers
           the pollen
                the blooming

washed
through the mud vein
deep within the earth
      the sand histories
      the animal swarms

enter the big liquid eyes
into the empty arena

tiny comes the spark
heavy comes the feeling
catching
    alight
        inside the skull

the secrets of nature
    world
        after
           world
              remembering

I am the grain
    and the desert
I am the drought
    and the seed
I am the travelling parts
and surrender solitude
to become free

these memories

and these wounds
no piece
of me
is mine
                        even
                        the dust atom
                        in the eye
                        is borrowed

IV

Salt in the Wounds
Opens the Heart Eyes

trick of the light

I
see
in
you

as
I
see
in
me.

just like flowers
reflect
the colours
they don't absorb,

we reflect
the shadows
of
our wounds.

take out on the couch

parade the room,
angel escape,
twirling swirling bomb.
watching you move there
in little black undies
bends my organs.

when will the Japanese arrive?

holographic skin,
firelight,
hungry alien,
hewn from some starry outcrop.

we wait together,
flicking through the channels,
escaping the abuse of sunlight—
and on the tv
in Pompeii
unearthed,
two bodies entwined,
starving
or horny
or fearful of the end.
just apes
together
passing the time.

there are less grand farewells…

and every second,
more like them,
more like us,
alone together
quivering like arrows.

and every minute,
it's our last chance
to grasp the hush,
       the bone,
       the blood
and drive the flame into the lake.

so we ignore the door
and crawl under the blanket once more
while the delivery driver
waits outside…

we can only record the times
in which we live

white sage
and the burning myrrh,
orange poppies
in a green field,
clean sheets on the string line
trying to escape in the wind.

I drink my beer in the sunshade
and watch my little bird
humming away
with afternoon laundry.

bra in one hand,
peg in the other,
silk knickers hugging her peach.

there is no better assembly of world…

I have never understood
the useless yearning for another life.

the colours
and shadows
that settle here:
      virgin,
and for a hair span, live
           undisturbed.

no one else will breathe here—
and maybe one day,
the witness will warp
or fade in retelling.
but right now,
there is no reckoning;
these moments stay uncorrupted

and are what they truly are:
                    fleeting.

and to future men,
automatic doors
and electric cigarettes
might offer a wholesome tease.

they will say
"oh, to be alive back then…"
and
"I was born in the wrong era."

and though
the roaring twenties
appeal to me
and the speakeasies of old.

they were not given to me to know…

only a glimpse
across times divide
by those
who have sacrificed
and cast their lives out
like nets
to leave silhouettes
that show bare
the trappings
of the soul.

and however pleasurable
it is to reminisce,
they cannot belong to us.

our duty

is to our impermanence.

how many stay vacant
and un-bloomed
wishing for other moments,
              other guests
instead
of the spectacular now?

we are spectators
of a rare odyssey

and we can only record
the times
in which we live.

the lake

beneath two palms,
behind black aluminium doors
in the dark,
we can hear the swans
moving across time—

angel-white chariots
floating peacefully
above their ebony tomb.

they return here
despite the hellish crusade.
nature provides
to delete them;
they still return to one another,
following only the trails
long hidden in the ancient dream.

are we like them
without choice
or do our paths
lay uncertain?

did I find you again
only to talk of dead stars
as if they still live
and wait in carparks
as the almost
make louder the silence?

what horrors we revive:
those hook-clawed beasts,
running wild through the corridors
of our before,
making us resist our own migrations

and so...
if life is lived mostly in memory,
then my faith in choice declines.
the mind seems to be a poor compass,
and if hearts should not be wasted,
then it is touch that remains true.

only our bodies
can provide us
with this brief respite.

worm food

when
we
wake
in the morning,
we have rolled the dice
and won.

even when there is
blood on the leaves,
stains on your trousers,
dead car batteries
and
overdue rent,
we are lucky.

one hundred million
bastards
didn't
get
the
egg—

didn't form the soul,
didn't pass through the orgasm
to be greeted by the sun,
by the body
with their very own
morsel of time
in the cosmic solution.

all of this
on a chance…

a blue drag
in the footsteps outside
impales me.

the people,
the people,
THE PEOPLE
wasted!

always hovering
just above
the thin line
of alright.

I would say to those
trapped in the glass house:
pick up a stone.

question your reality
and you will find
it is most fragile…

cherchez la femme

press play!

enter summer deluge:
olives
on the tongues of the young.
tender loss
happens quickly.
listening to dead heroes
and laying siege
to southern skies.
now birds, I cannot name.
look for the blood in me;
they will never find it.
it feigns promise
like some strange scarlet echo
into the bosom of the hills
just as the sun
        not quite sun above
undoes
the powerlines
and antennae
who were built without choice,
and asks
the asphalt to return
slowly to its beginning sum.
I realise
I am no longer wholly mine.

to be unmade
in the arms of another:

        a most freeing deceit.

and I forgive
just as hornets
don't know they are cruel.

    I denounce this crime.

I hope this never ends
between you and me.
I hope we merge
and forget
we were
two.

infirmity

white lilies
in a blur,
horses and houses
turning to dust—
she is gone.

nothing can be done about it...

on a driveway
a woman tends to a handsome cat
who is sunbathing like a genius.
he is handled
and stroked
and saved
whilst I pick up dresses
and dirty underwear off the floor.

what a terrible joke!
this city has too many clowns already.
we need more uncertainty
and cliffs to jump from
and cars turning around and coming home,
because there is so little time;
some see it in tea leaves.
others don't see it at all—
and meanwhile
                      out there,
                      out there
the angels want fair pay,
predators line the Vatican,
rock stars drop like flies,
modern women
with cross bows
shoot down the patriarchy,
and the plastic bottle kills the world.
                      out there,

                    out there...
in here,
in here
last night's chinese
spins in the microwave
and I see the sorrow in the almost-heaven.
all I want
is for someone
to help chase
the shadows away...

portals

home
from
work.
late is the hour.
tired,
I strip:
the clothes,
the socks,
the meat,
the bones
and throw what's left in the bed—
and as ritual,
I travel
through the pale-black sheer
into the cracked-roof cornice
stairway
to the pie in the sky.

portals to you will never die here;
doorways overlayed
in a single mass constellation.

and here I am:
jumping through,
breaching the flood
like a puppeteer
dancing with these counterfeit apparitions.

across the night,
rainbows appear in prison cells,
a storm cloud passing
over the dried sheets of the Mojave,
and I lay
for thirty or forty minutes more like this
until I am completely
destroyed.

to the people in horror row

do not let a good thing die;
there is time yet,
there are still blueberries
with cream
and mysteries
with fat legs and things to teach you.

so, let them cut you down,
arborists of the soul,
and show mornings
are behind the curtain.
do not let it slip away.
there is failure to attend;
you must delete
and re-emerge above ruin encountered.

there is always a way out—
beyond the scourge of the mind,
beyond columns that support finality.
you are not alone.

we are temporary earth.
run,
seek the wild.
there are trains that wait for you a thousand times
and lead to some small measure of peace.

do not let a good thing die;
there is time yet,
and the sun
will
rise
again.

black tobacco
navy blue

do not remember me;
I have done little harm,
I leave with lands unknown,
      bodies untouched,
      words unspoken,
virgin ideas pulled up from the internal well
unexposed—
and private worlds doomed heavily,
forgotten.

so many books
and their quiet resources abandoned
as waves of sound
      taste
      truth and horror,
die alongside,
flirt down hallways
of pleasures I will never know…

such price I pay
to mourn them in the mind field:
escaped potentials,
collectively unharmed,
taken and locked away by time's keeper.

such cruelty to hold on,
such freedom to ignore.
what nonsense do many endure
entirely of our own creation?
      crucified largely by things unborn
      and paths that will never be…

in any sense,
there are tigers here
in the long un-mowed grass.

I smile at them
and walk on by.

to live in a constant state of annihilation
is to know that grief and joy
are one in the same.

there will be no solidity in my story
and no certainty in my stride;
it is human to remain incomplete.

nomadicy is man's true advantage.
I live to be changed,
moved in someway—
nothing more or less demanded:
        a passer-by
        in this rare
        delight.

V

Like Incense Burning Away

magnum opus

someday,
we will all sleep
in a raven-coloured tomb.

and while breath is hot
and the idea alive,

we have
one
of two
choices:

to ripen
or
to rot.

what's the matter, benny?

spitting
out
the last of my sun.

what's the point?

blue fox,

you think
you know
the answers,
but
you don't.

you have summoned
the mountains
by only
imagining their peaks,

depriving the journey
of what gives it substance.

no wonder
you feel
like a stranger to the world.

in your arrogant
and infant knowledge,
you believe
you can script
the outcomes
so you don't even begin.

routine
and prejudice distort your vision.

you are waiting
for something,
for someone,
for anything
to beat the numbness.

the S.O.S beacons
come back empty-handed.

why shouldn't they?
when you only send parcels
of personal agony,
no more invitations.

as
an Egyptian
or Greek
or gryphon
once said:
    each person
    believes their own horizon
    is the end of the world.

perception
is reflection.

the one thing
you avoid
is the one thing
that will
save you:

authentic participation.

blue fox,

you converse
with so little
of the world
and still ask why
it understands
so little
about
you...

don't shoo away the butterfly

no suffering
is done alone
so the ground suffers drought,
the flowers wilt,
the colours fade,
the man dies a little inside.

hungry hippos

we eat life
from the toes up,
learning to walk and talk
love and lie,
fuck and fall over—
and by the time we get to the head,
we are too full of the little things
to see the big one.
we solidify in life
and become blind to its message
and lack the fluidity to be free.

are we too proud
to admit
we were fools once?
young impressionable fools
fumbling around,
trying to make sense of it all,
learning how to cope with pain.

the sad thing is
most of us remain so
for the duration of our lives.
though some of us survive,
a daring few
who put our pain into a thing:
a doing
       a service
              a creation—
some remnant that there was hope
and dreams within.
we cough up art
and turn the odds
with a stamp on time.
by this measure,
we cheat death.

eels in the creek

nothing truly ends.
everything is reborn:
every death brings new life,
every ending is a new beginning.
goodbyes are a false ideal.

everyone meets again
on the planes of life,
between the doors of death,
in the halls of memories,
in the tears of the soul.

venus lake

I waited
and waited
while the hordes outside consume,
while the pendulum swings.

I waited
like a dog by the door—
and just like that,
she came back to me
and brought her tiny white stars;
members
of the cult,
of beauty.
and after some bleeding,
we sat alone
at the kitchen table,
holding each other,
laughing in technicolour,
talking and eating
Vietnamese takeout
from a local restaurant.

I admire the chef;
their art
is never immortal.

it belongs only to present comforts.

I wonder now:
who can last?

perhaps
Giza's three,
jellyfish
or the rose of Jericho…

all cold things
all unrelatable.

to be passionately alive
is to embrace the temporary.

we can promise nothing
of tomorrows
and we may never
hold each other again,
but right now,
her and I
burn brightly
as we were made.
and loving
with such quality
has no fear
of time.

we are old
and we are young

three
thousand
miles
cross-country
searching for the perfect spot.

she packed bread and oil
and I forgot
the map.

and after four hours
of arguing,
we ended up in pastoral farmland.

and under a white flag,
off ripped the shirts,
the pants,
the stockings,
the bra.

her legs up on the dash
like a stringless marionette
and I, entangled on my knees,
performed somewhat like prayer.

most seek it
in silk sheets,
in Indian heat—
not the front seat
in a field like this.

but the day had no chains
and the air
tasted like salt and gasoline
and sunlight on the tall grass.

and like Hollywood lovers
half-undone,
we carved our names
into an oak tree
to stand rogue
on the hill
as a future relic.

and these memories,
a bunch of renegades
that will
burn,
burn,
burn
my body
to remember:

there is infinite time
in youth
if you plan
on having
an infinite youth.

freak show

big
bang
star
seeds
volcanic
eruptions
reptilians
deadly comets
ice ages
and woolly mammoths
shrubbery
mud huts
fire-taming
tool-making
tree-cutting
sounds that became symbols
symbols that became words
kings and queens
engines and empires
aqueducts
witch hunts
religious dogma
horse-riders
gun powder
seafaring
government expansion
law-making
war
and more law-making
protesting
bra burnings
nuclear energy
missiles
and slaughter houses
the apocalypse farms
cell phones

computers
the electric toothbrush
microwave meals
window wipers
solar panels
chemtrails
space travel
and
drones

what the fuck…

all
of
that

just so
I can experience
temporary peace
driving through
a street puddle
on my way home?

am I supposed to
laugh
in the acid rain

to electrify
each day

and indulge
in the absurdity?

maybe
to remove our shelters,
to remain a little soft

and make joy
in the small things
is to avoid
death
in
life.

this is something.

maybe this means something…
maybe this means nothing at all.

the longest days must have end

let me tell you:
I've met angels in the flesh
and they certainly don't have wings;
      they walk alongside the truth.
I've known workers too:
suits and the soulless,
runaways and the damned,
people bent and twisted,
poisoned with regret
who keep names
like relics in a graveyard—
the kind who need a nail in the hands
to hold them down,
make them see,
make them bleed.

they don't see anything
and they don't feel anything.
instead, they walk on by
like a ghost in their lives.

I understand what it's like
to be an enemy to living
and blame the external noise
for the inside noise.
but you're the only one yelling.

if you want to go back,
you can't.
it's gone!
so, move forward
and put that anger into something good.

you have so much in you it's gone silent.
I can hear it:
that deafening silence.

when you hear it too,
take a shotgun to your life;
blow that shit up
spit on its grave,
piss on the tombstone,
look at what it has done to you,
and after the fog clears,
do something for yourself,
fight for yourself!

if you are breathing, nothing is lost—
and if you can't... try again
because self-loathing is outdated.
it's boring, it's a copout, it's for wannabes.

I scorn the cowardice in self-destruction.
self-love is for the revolutionary;
it's the only way you are going to find
truth in this place.

and the truth is:
we are not here to end suffering;
we are here to master it.

VI

The Comings and Goings of Night Trains

never mind the name of it

if found,
never return;
it is done
and we are made
of strange power.
there are holes in me,
and when I water them down,
it goes right through
like a weevil in rye.

strange power:
kings,
slaves,
sages,
the antenna man,
his daughter,
the woman who cuts her hair—
all stifling mad with it
at least once.

the taste never leaves us:
the deep sour of divinity.

strange power…
I feel it
when my skull is in my hands
and the brain is soft
and I have said too much,
drunk too much,
feared too much.

your image leaks into me,
and I am there again
in that place we belong,
where ardour resides
and youth lives on.

strange power…
I was doomed from the start.
you will always
be the flame
and I,
the moth.

in the forest

haven,
her body was;

a portal
to the inner man.

and in her shade,
I found grace
amongst
the agony.

tango

what lies
on the lips
cannot be solved alone,
only
uncovered,
and by another
transforms
into a rush
of grace
that oscillates
over the body
in orchestral heat.

these muscles remain useless;
its chambers without song
if not
for our lovers
and their sublimity…

in the morning,
in the day,
in the night,
they strike gently
and do reveal
a kiss
is not
a kiss
until it is shared
upon your lips.

equals

colours of union
backwashed against the bedding
like great art watered out.
yesterday's song
          survived.

and though the hours have past
and the leftovers in the fridge grown colder,
I am
still warm
for you.

      despite reused jokes
      and the post between
      and pigeons on tiles
      and the horrendous sun.
still
      the barricades
                burn
                        down.

somehow, the melody won.

we have spent the day
lounging,
foraging,
defeating one another.

and now,
the timing is late
and the moths die out
to cruel blue flames
      and all the people
      in bed
      are sleepy
and in the corner

of some old ruin,
the sound of sweet surrender:
    your skin
    on my skin,
your body moving beneath mine.
how can
bones
    and flesh
rubbing together
make such music?

sad anime

there are two paths
in every argument:
a telephone
and a loaded gun.

perhaps we could have been saved…

instead,
the taxi
makes its way
far from here
into the steel woods,
the super cluster
the permanent fog.

and ribbons of wind
streak rain upon the glass;
there is no longer a face
looking back.

and the eventual sound
the city made—
its breath
and boil—
was akin
to the mumblings
of wild men
saddled by demons.

poet

are
you
at
peace?
sad eyes
made
of stone.

the more you feel,
the less you know.

expansion
is
the
eater
of innocence.

it is
what
fumigates
the lost

and by
consequence,
excuses,
the sloths
and the scutoids
that behead
reality
and suck the joy.

the climbing,
the churning,
the snipping at each other's
tendons—

yet
there is something
more terrifying
than pathless
movement…

it lies
outside the fragile shield
in the empty vacuum of space,
in the cold
and tasteless darkness
that most
don't want to face.

you must face it.

cradle your enemies
because there are no enemies.

accept this always,
accept this always.

expel polarity,
remove judgement,
look to the deep road—
beyond belief,
beyond the science
and explaining of things.

look
to where
the light gets in.

look to the spells
we place on each other
despite the need

for reproduction

there is something there…

beyond that,
beyond the cellular,
beyond the gears of clocks,
inside the internal fire.

this is where you will find it.

custodian…

witness
the pulling
between all living things
and in the motion
sickness.
be aware of your difference;
it is your lens,
it is your gift
to defend
the seams
that connect us all.

do not popularise the mockery of hope.

we
are
all
we have
                      out here.

accept this always
in the alleys
of the cities of men,

in the silence of tree herds
amongst the bombs of war.

we are all we have.

wherever you go,
accept this truth.

only with these eyes
and only from this channel
will you be able to hear
the consummate sounds of the age.

unfortunately

fortune favours the fortunate.
the rest of us
have to take what we want
with swollen hands
and heavy eyes.

and if you want it,
it is yours,
but be prepared
to pay a lifespan for it.

if it is vital to your being,
it is worth any price.

feathers on the wind

I would like to think
there is a place for us,
but we are feathers on the wind.

although
I may never have her heart,
I can give her solace
for a time
with a glass of red,
some warm bread and oil,
and good conversation.

and if there is a bed
by her requests,
then this temporary thing
can become an immortal one
in the space between our memories.

out of our control

eucalyptus trees,
dead cats
on the
road—

or maybe
they are birds…

who knows?
no turning back.

hands on the wheel.

the street signs
are all bent,
scratched and graffitied.
no one wants to remember their names.

around
every corner
in every neighbourhood,
there is a sorrowful side
to season's end.

it is in the moving on.

it's in the twisting leaves
falling like rain in the breeze,
left behind
to perish
by the trees
who have forgotten them.

I know
deep down
it is

the crossing,
the sacred,
the necessary.

yet I cannot shake the disappointment:

cunning as a cat,
delicate as a bird—
we are all eventual roadkill.

and like damaged
street signs
and worn out leaves,

we are to be used
by others
or become useless.

but what we are
what we become
in the stories
of others
is not for us
to decide…

to decay
in the autumn
of their minds.

what appears cruel
is
actually
passage.

VII

Urban Birds

VII

ignorance isn't bliss
its betrayal

A one
hundred
year
goodbye.

man is an ant on a blade of grass
spinning towards the exit.

the clocks are falling,
pulled down by monkeys and their free wi-fi.
on islands of tyres burning,
swans float
       legs up—
ivory white
mutilated
       unready
like coral bleached.
only the towers stand like gravestones,
remembering something of the forests.
there is apocalypse
everywhere a man
can breathe…

"catastrophe!"
I yell
at the enemy
in the mirror.

slowly
we advance
like a shy bride
into
the chrominance of man.

a catastrophe!

there still remains something wild in me;
I save the moth in the toilet
and piss dutifully
on the citrus tree
and reject denialism
and rejoice in the rain.
                it is not enough.

and still
        she remains
resilient:
        electric blue heaven.
we wait on the calvary together
at the foot of the gibbet
and I cannot bear to tell her
that the world
always arrives
when it is fashionably
too late…

tips and tricks
(at the writers' conference)

the speaker
needs
to have
a clean environment
and tries to get it down
in tune with her natural cycles;
understanding the body's law
is very important for maximum
efficiency.

the next one
must have clear skies
and find himself
in a park
an open space;
somewhere he can receive
God's message.

another
bearing resemblance
to hessian
and the cults of India
suggested guided meditation
and mornings
adamantly—
no
later
than
twelve!

the old boy
next to me
with balls
of molten lava
rumbled

"I've never heard of any of you…"

"most of fishing is sitting there waiting for a bite."

and then went on
to tell us
it comes to him
in the evening hours
to music—
Bach preferably—
and his wife
makes him
hot English tea.

and they didn't
even
ask me…

nevertheless,
I must be milked
Orion's belt—
ought to be aligned.
the Gulf of Carpentaria
must receive
three consecutive weeks
of rain.
and if it's not too much trouble,
I desire
the bottled
perfumed
fart
of
Demeter.

there are people
so consumed

with the process
they don't get anything done.

bushfires

the weekly sour:
I brush my teeth with it.
I read them:
their faces.

today's politicians,
poor animated things
thrown from the hive
a handful at a time—
strung up,
ribbons and scissors,
second-hand smoke—
with their first inaugural breath.

it's terrible
and absent of folly.
real people
have to get up
and keep the cities from burning.
real people
have to squeeze the last
of the toothpaste
and pull lung
and hair
from the sink
and find sunrise
ugly
at least once…

when disaster strikes,
we are the reaction
to what we can't control.

words are made strong
by those behind them.
to lead

is a promise.

where is the sacrality
in our vows to one another?
are we so far removed from the tribe?

those up on the podiums
turn on the sanctimony.
have they no shame?

now the neighbours fear dead grass
and one billion animals die
in the fires of home—
and one billion more
will die tomorrow
on the plates at brunch.

there is too much death.
too much!
where is the pitchfork and scythe?

and while the prime minister
jets off to Hawaii,
I pour a can of beans into a bowl,
zap for sixty seconds,
flip the newspaper over,
and look for the stars.
maybe they will uphold
their promise…

I suppose the mob
was ruined the day
the tv was born,
and now revolution
is just the movement
in a microwave.

death to a parisian cliché

I know those people
over there.
I pity those people;
people like them
put locks on bridges.
        they don't know love,
        they don't know shit.
you can't lock it down;
it's a sham.

you were both wild once;
it's such a goddam shame.
now you laugh less,
behave more.
it is sad to watch
the domestication of fire…

good friday
(in isolation)

mercury's
in retrograde:
unemployment rising,
stock markets plummeting,
world leaders shitting themselves,
eight-hundred dead in a day.

healthcare workers
in hazmat suits.
refrigerator trucks,
now make shift morgues.

aged care clusters.
elbow handshakes,
toilet paper shortages,
supermarket brawls.

take away eating,
video game meeting,
online screening,
internet porn.

body weight workouts,
government bailouts,
celebrity opinions,
welfare lines.

big bank sympathies,
viral conspiracies,
facemasks,
rubber gloves,
vaccine calls.

pray to antibodies;
anybody—

Buddha, Allah, Horus, Hashem,
Odin, Jesus, Zeus, Amaterasu—
whilst the planet takes a breather
like an infected lung.

the only virus
I see
is the human one.

one point five metres from resuming…

tomorrow:
wet markets,
dog meat festivals,
pangolin murder,
sunbear bile.

it's the East,
not us.
condemn them,
sue them.
drive on through
to happy meals,
bacon stacks,
supersized bucket wings
and plastic-wrapped beef.

slavery is prettier to look at
in the lands of the free.

world eaters,
your money is your vote.

be wary
of those
who only fight

for one cause;
all oppression is linked.

because everything
everywhere
is connected.
ask one man
and a bat…

masters and meal tickets

under
the rifle tower,
and
the chopping block,
we populate
the factory exhibit.

hours
and hours
hunched over
between fluorescent tubes together,

my fellow compadres
move
with the efficiency
of
precise machines.

after years of service,
the spirit dislocates
and there, begins a longing
for the outside external
like bees
buzzing against a window.

but they can no longer remember
the external
or what to do with it.
the external has become a fabula;
we talk of it mythologically.
imagine it.
imagine the lottery and its fortunes.
laugh and live
in the lie…

day in

and day out,
they continue to smile
despite
our small chance
of escape.

although
I'm planning
to break out
and will leave them
and never look back,
I cannot help
but love them now.

their hellish refuge,
colour rays
in the repetitive grey,
the working people—

somehow,
their humanity
remains

like an oasis
in the desert:

concealed
but not
lost.

pemberton party

there is a wind song
petrified
in the night-time trees
compounded
into the illusion
of breath.

these
old
pickled
souls
form a cathedral
on the hillside.

the vapour
from country rain
rises amongst them—
almost holy
in the moonlight.

in their minds:
that shimmering gossip.
they are sad
for our short
little lives
but
I pity them most.

they are already at the altar
and request nothing of the night.

they cannot travel to each other
and taste the hallelujah

or see
what music writes

with restless legs
who move
with such urgency
in the dark rooms
of youth.

and if God
made the muscles,
then passion
sought their fame.

perhaps
it is
the liquid courage,
the wooden skeletons burning
or
the brief
forgetting
of sunrise
that make our nights
fragile
and bleed
in
electric
honesty.

even though I'm not confident
with the language
and I'm not a dancer
or a saint,
I can still
feel their joy
spinning
around
the red fire,
the cruel flowers,

the embarrassed landscapes.

I could sit
on the couch
for hours
like this
reading the Holocene.

I could stare wide
admiring
the alive

until their bodies
fall
around me
like collapsing
engines.

VIII

The Tugging Shapes of Sky

images that last

I
ache
for
nowhere
else:

eating
cool
grapes
on a
warm bed
of
grass.

my gorgeous
blonde
baby
and her friends
swimming
and walking around
in
stringy
things.

the glass surface of the lake,
the total absence of wind,
the shimmering sunlight.

nature
and women
nature
and women
like
churches
designed
to intimidate

peasants.

I am learning
to appreciate
the rock:

the threshing young,
the handsome ugly,
the winsome old.

hunks of meat
hurling through space,
the pleasing moods
of a pale
blue
dot.

orion's belt

midnight
car ride
alongside
the
blue-black
sauvignon:

the photo on the dash
wildly alive,

the dancing Gabriel,

St Christopher around my neck
                              gold,

the music
like honey dashed against the rocks,

the great
deep
grumble of waves.

the light beam on the road,
a million
galactic sun spores.

the scarlet
      digital a.m. clock,
blood fire rubies
      ticking over.

all parallel
to thoughts of you…

fractals

on
the
toilet
seat
not
quite
so
alone

above
a
palomino
horse
grazes
on
a
field
of
wild
daises

no pressure…

there
are
better horses
better men
      in bathrooms
      in oxeye fields
trying to scratch
the elusive itch

and it
always
comes out
in parts

very rarely
does it
come out
whole

but it will come
eventually

by a splash
        a thunder
a torrential rain
to
piddle
down
and lubricate
the masses

hundreds
don't even notice
its passing

though
to the trained
and the patient,
it's almost better
than the orgasm.

almost…

"no pushing!
you can't
force it."
chuck jones says.

listen!
pay attention

to the line.

but after
fifteen minutes
sitting here
and staring at this horse,
I'll be happy
if either one of us
dumps
a single stroke
on the portrait
of
chaos.

kintsugi

scaffolding
on the Pantheon,
oculus in the sky,
two thousand years
of weather,
cocktails of gods
and unheard prayer.

forget the carver's names,
the benefactors,
the emperors who ruled.

the stone knows nothing
of the country it was hauled from;
how it was handled,
how it was changed.

the burnings,
the history deleted,
the history saved,
the agreed upon fables.

the more we survive,
the more is added to our intrinsic value.
like ancient temples,
our souls are built,
not born whole.

what should be worshipped in us?

this place
       a feeling.

             there are no permanent wounds;
             there is only healing.

what remains holy in us
is in
our constant state
of repair.

supernatural cathedral woman

rainfall heavy,
soggy roses,
blood in my brow,
rolling
      rogue
           thunder
to a
blue
dying sky.

spirit of the night;
clarity
is coming.

she visits us
in lightning flashes.

supernatural
cathedral
woman
who lives
form free
and hallowed
amongst
the wild birds
in the salt winds
above the ocean.

and as long as
we are in attendance
tonight,
tomorrow,
someday,
somehow

she will come

as the silk waves
of time
wash over us.

her ancient reveal,
like a mind breath.

her gothic voice
like a salve
on the wounds
of the soul.

art is quite useless
and absolutely necessary

I can feel it humming
through the September trees,
growing through any man
obscure
        cinematic
                sawdust.
I grasp only a little
until
it performs again
through ventriloquist apparatus:
the lone cartoonist,
the crying babe,
and the wink of whores.
it is there
ancient in the millennia shells,
a part of the cobblestone war,
against the palm oil thongs
who terrorize
and sculpt this city anew.

they are all
       just because
it is all
       just because…

same
       same
but different.
everything so easily understood
yet
so hard to define.

ageless
       infectious
calling like a random door

in the middle of the desert.

Picasso saw it too
in the particle dust
of the studio light.

Baret
in the sea spray mists
on her quest for the unknown.

Delvigne
in the bullet.

Achilles
in the immortal blade.

anywhere you go
through history:
                wormhole
                        and lock
it's the same
        same
        but different.

to some, it hounds.
to others, a whisper.
some die from it;
those who cannot face it.
and others
over-saturate their attempts.
some get close—
closer than most.
though nobody
can "science it"
completely.

the greatest haunting of man
fractured a million a piece;
we are joined in our non-discovery.

and yet, it still ripples
in Cecilia Payne's star laws,
in Cohen's hallelujah,
and Mandela's cry for freedom,
in the first fire crackle
of the atomic dream.

our lives are all linked impossibly.

the capture:
it is we who pass the torch.

little by little
        life by life
brushes
        instruments
                telescopes
spatulas
        inkwells
                brains
hands out wide—
all leaning into
the infinite breeze.

IX

Door Knocking

chastity belt

woke up
full of life,
full of teeth,
full of sperm
and wrote a list
of October sins
(like the good sheep that I am)
and one hundred and thirty profanities.

I tore them up
and a blind dog ate the pieces.
and a coffee
two cigarettes
and some half-burnt marmalade toast
shot the dog.

the next hour,
I walked down church street
and pissed on a fire hydrant
next to a starship Jesus
who was waiting for change
as I wait for genius without stimulants.

all I can think about
is that the bees deserve a proper burial
and the saints and their nimbuses,
stubborn as stone,
renounce the miracle of nature
and deploy annunciation.

how different we are:
some of us
feel the shape of eternity
and laugh as we hold each other
and some of us
turn into bronze

copper statues
with urban birds
shitting down
the backs of our necks.

membership revoked

the
first
time
I walked
into a church
and
saw
Jesus
Christ
hanging there,
he took
my crown
of
thorns.

he asked me
to free him

and
told me
to pity those
who only think
in terms
of bounty.

I spent years
trying to get the bastard out
but
being the main attraction,
they had him
by the hands
and feet.

so, I returned my immunity
and don't go back anymore.

the price is too high,
too many Sundays lost
to layby,
a heaven.

the costumes frightened me.

and I was always unsure
if the priest
was giving me the eye…

now
I water
the rosebuds
for the sake
of blooming

and figured
we all eventually
end up
on the cross

if the mountain
is the mountain,

there are many ways
to the top.

I prefer my roads
a little
less
embalmed

even if
it is
paved

with thorns.

follow the heart and you'll never go wrong
follow the mind and you'll live comfortably

along the homebound road
between the narrow trees,
the flickering sunlight gold
morsecode of Anael—
her message easily undone
reblooms within
a knowing
that was always there…

maestro

the end
is nigh.

the path
to inner peace
is in fifteen minutes
or less—
money back
guaranteed!

two-dollar
burgers,
fifty meters
down the road.

my letter box gags
on pamphlets
of seduction.

they always want
the soul
or money
or dictatorial devotion.

the first,
I cannot yield
and
unfortunately,
my wallet is empty
and
I have already been persuaded
inside the temple of a woman.
      I know what worship is.

this one says
they will feed the hungry.

I am quite
peckish…

I start my car
and look for loose change
between the grubby leather seats,
praying for a miracle buck—

to get on one's knees
and suck the cock of God
hoping he will lend you a five…

if the great author
is within us
like most
of the ancient texts
and advertisements say,
then prayer
is not a question,
it is a command

and we must proceed
with action.

turn left,
then a right
at the roundabout:
the golden arches
are on the corner.

nightfall

when eternity knocks,
I feel you near—
inside,
outside
the world is burning.

the circles
of our lives
are parting

and the great black mass
of unknowing
divides me.

unknown to the dreams you have,
unknown to the visions you see.

I could only hope
to appear in one:

in the corner,
in the backdrop,
in the replay.

so, when your eyes open
and you reach for morning,
you'll find me in your first thought
like something lost,
someone missed.

dancing in the dirt

I often feel like the only observer,
and everyone else participates.
I feel alone in my thoughts
and sharing them is futile
because no one understands
the shade of mind
I've been walking in
my entire life.
I don't either…

I look to the healers,
the preachers,
these great sods in silky tatters,
glorified salesmen—
and their wisdom is lost on me.
they tell me how to be a good man,
but I'm a villain like everybody else.
they tell me what I can do
to come to their afterparty,
but I don't like what they sell;
it's all too flimsy for me.

eternal happiness…
they use it like a lure.
even the Greeks have their orgies
and I don't do groups.
they sell happiness when it's too late—
for the price of death,
for the price of saying no to life's pleasures.
they can keep their heavens,
and I'll have mine here.
I prefer life.

the sad,
gritty
ancient beast;

he tells good jokes.
we laugh together at his false designs
and my poor choices.
we are just as unsure as each other.

I don't want to die.
not now, not yet—
nor wear the white frock of purity
and wine and dine at heaven's course.
instead,
give me the eternal promise
here on earth
in this colourful blood,
in this forgiving soil
with my hands full of words
and their precious, vicarious music.

what a fortunate mistake it is to live!

if I can't have that,
there's always reincarnation…
I'll come back as a door,
watching the people walk hand in hand
with their hopes
and their problems—
interesting enough
an observer again.

and maybe
I'll have something new
to write about…

witch hunts

they hold placards
outside
the centres
yelling
at the girls
going in.

sometimes they spit,
sometimes they read a psalm too
whilst
somewhere
in the suburbs,
their
adolescent sons
continue
their pilgrimage,
spreading
the
legs
of
God.

at least
they are making full use
of the perks of membership…

      a little confession,
      a dash of holy water,
      some repetitive penance

      and voilà!

            absolution.

they can feel
better

about things
like hating homosexuals,
wanking to dirty films,
denying a woman's choice,
and calling Debbie
a bitch…

reach

an endless fury resides in me;
a stellar nightmare,
an impossible dream.
I am attracted
to what I don't understand,
which renders
me useless
to any sort of obedience.

and in the long
deep
tendrils of thought,
I hunger always
for an absent gold.

I ask Hypatia of her description,
I ask Kusama for her eyes,
I ask Rachmaninoff and his long fingers
and pedigree ass,
I ask Bukowski and his bottles,
      Ginsberg and his arresting howl,
      Sagan and his starward gaze,
      Rodriguez and the streets of Detroit,
      Monroe and her consuming tease
           and intelligent trailblazing heart.

one
by
one,
I devour them all
and don't waste a drop of blood.

the elusiveness of its touch
grants each of us
a romance with faith.

and we all carry within us;
an unrepeatable signature

to face the road alone,
to carry the anchors alone,
to brave the world alone.

and if
the meaning is never to be found,
we still prevail…

what courage
to let loose the whispers of one's heart
and walk the path
despite an absolute—

to leave behind an authentic step
in this electric blue fight
is a salute
of hope
for the human wild.

X

Russian Caravan

machines in the garden

bleed for me,
labyrinth unseen.
dance with me in the dark

in your arms,
the high ledge,
the pavement below.
it's the final promise
of the world

we are incense burning away...

what shall I do
with the crackling
electrical-storm brain,
the crippled beauty
of mountains,
the short-lived waves
at the end of land?

keep bleeding for me;
drown my horror
and do not leave
this bastard dry.

across the fall,
I will impart recordings,
simple toasts
to contend with forever.

we are made eternal
in the touch of others.
maybe even
death cannot
take us wholly
if we

scatter the pieces.

fear no endings
fear no odds

in the absence
of meaning,
the treasure is the road.

to witness
the lightning
in the heartbeat of a hummingbird

and watch the tree herds
expand slowly
like a liquid
over the valleys;

to share stories
and bodies
backseat
under the copper sundowns
and violet rains
on the highways of Australia;

to taste the spit
       breath
         and blood
of the holy ghosts
who vibrate
their way
into the heart-fields
like wild horses;

to wander down streets
where the shadows weep
and hear the composers
who make music
with the silence
of God.

how arrogant
it is to believe
there is only one
path for you.

an answer,
a cure-all.

burn it away!

there are a million
different ways
to exist out here
on the road.

*the road
is calling.*

to be found
in any sense,
one
must first
get
lost.

eyes of the undine

green neons
across the bar
like pickled sunlight.
river moss
in a jade jar.
just green to end.
the end.

that's why
exit signs are green;
they are the last colour
you see before going blind.

portugal

I've lost thirty dollars
this afternoon
sitting on a
       (not entirely uncomfortable)
apple crate
sharing a bottle of ginja
and playing dice
with the men in the square;
they have smoked all my cigarettes.
I don't mind;
I enjoy their company.

we do not share
the same language.
instead,
back and forth,
we laugh
at our attempts
and point at things
both ugly and divine.

the cathedral scowls
at these old hounds
and a pup
and welcomes multiple
crazed romantics
hunting for something
brag-able
to take home
and decorate their suburban excuse.

I pretend I am different from them
and try to blend in
as I watch the cold stone
crack under the floor of their cameras.
a pink-glazed sun

swept up from Africa
makes it all seem
postcard-pretty.

all this history:
buildings and locals
suntanned with it
yet
        ever
so
        present

and the future belongs somewhere else;
it continues
and I chew
another sickly sour cherry.

and we point
        and point
        and laugh
        in vain
hoping that it will remove
the small space between us.
they will do this again tomorrow.
I will remember them,
but they will forget me…

call the muses home

there is gold
in the light
of a stolen
glance.

I forget
the corruption
in me.

I've never
given much
thought to the organs
but
they
bend
to
your
names.

when you go
wherever it is
people like you go,
they
are
pulled
by
the shape
of your absence.

contender

test of the spirit,
ravine of the brain.
life has a danger
that a shelter will never know.

the passage
to any form of enlightenment
comes to those
who confront
the terrible darkness.

all goes that way
at some point
and eventually,
for all of us.

if one means to know themselves
and experience all shades of the world,
suffering is built
into the structure of existence.

you will encounter it
many times over;
this is certainty
and fear will come to greet you.
do not hide.
it is not everything;
it is not absolute.
dig deep.
you have a thousand reasons inside you;
human capacity is an endless well.

be a fool,
befriend failure.
you will learn
not all defeat is loss.

just as not all joy is sustained,
there too will be times
of temporal happiness
and brief spells of ecstasy.
cherish them in the valley of the mind,
but do not seek them out.
you will grow little from this;
they will come freely,
accompanying a pursuit of something deeper.

do not abandon your evolution.
sail into the storm that looms;
the only way out lies within.
and if you must destroy the external,
annihilate the known.
go forth with haste;
time is precious
and idleness is the killer of dreams,
the invisible noose of a comfortable disease.

it is necessary to pause,
recoup and revitalise
to escape lethargic pull.
although indolence is cowardice
and the quiet murder of your potential.
it is giving up without admitting you are
the gas leak you refuse to fix.

it is not easy to look
in the unforgiving mirror
and scrape away the rust of negligence,
yet it must be done
for we are not supposed to live
stationary lives.

take me on a joy ride
in the countryside

death of a planet,
dreams of the sun,
the moving herds
strange flowers from the east,
the black
blue
lace of the marshes,
the winding rivers at dawn,
the cold wild sea air,
the red-burnished cheeks,
the single tear,
the last gold of the evening tide,
the final goodbyes,
the falling rockets,
the failed attempts,
the comings
and goings of night trains,
blood
and smoke
and bourbon
in the mouth,
grasses with patches of brown,
bent light through green-bottled glass,
the sea
and her prayers
as hands move above flames on the sand
searching for warmth.

thunder over the water,
storms in the heart,
the divination of women,
bodies that knock at the door.

the bewildering
names of places

      of people
of the worlds we travel to.
temples
on
Mars…

inspiration
is inertia

and only
the truth
can withstand ridicule.

perfection is ugly.

the broken
and desperate images
come like
foreign invaders
to my shore.

I will always
answer…

I am nothing more
than a
beggar
at the feet
of their beauty.

consider this a sign

keep walking!
avoid
the
tomb
at
all
costs.

bad luck
rises
like
subway air.

names
ache
and
then
they
don't.

show some mercy!
you have walked the difficult road
and earned the right to another sunrise.

keep walking.

you may not know the way,
but that doesn't mean there is no way.

and often
those who survive the jump,
the rope,
the excessive pill-taking
talk of regret
the moment
they stepped off.

keep walking.

most of us
don't really want
to kill ourselves;

we want to kill
something inside us.

this can be done
with help,
with time.

a thousand others
have come by this way
and leaned
over the edge of despair.

some have written down
exit maps
in the pages
of
millennia.

hear them out!

sometimes one line
can save you.

consider this a sign.

there are routes left
uncovered.

your pain
is a bridge

to others.

keep walking.

right now
that's all
you have to do.

amphoras

a fleeting pleasure,
a lasting pain.

this old weathered house
carries me to you.

veins on a young man's hand,
bottled
liquid whole.

walking down the street on fire,
tracing the heart lines.

to know you muddy,
to see and be seen,
to share our warm bodies,
unshackle the ghosts
and brave the hollow.

through countless strangers,
we have walked.

our twisting lives,
moving alongside
one another—
still unanswered.

darling,
there's a long
and winding road ahead.
would you stay
and walk
a little while?

XI

In Hindsight

fervour

love
is not beautiful;
it is poetry.
poetry is not beautiful,
it is a rose bush
that has been trodden on,
it is the lamp at the end of the tunnel collapsed,
it is the silt in the fibre
that clothes the wicked and the tamed.

it waits always
behind the switch in the laundry,
behind clenched muscles in their worship,
in night-crimes,
in the train tracks and the coal.

it is the dark enquiry
into worms and masses
and names beyond us,
it is the bird
outside the circus tent
where all the animals
pray until they are blind.

it is stitching unbloodied
and can be found
in crown upon crown colliding
with the fever of a star.

it is that ninety-nine percent
in a crowded room
and heard on a whisper of a promise.
it is the distant near,
the feeling of thunder after dark
and warm damp hands
over heat and brain

and flight and lion
and crotch on silk.

it is worth every spill and every stain,
it is insoluble,
it is forever,
it is more.
and in its blame,
it migrates the body
and gifts the mirror
to unmask
the true face of the soul.

blood pacts

we
were
so young…
how could we ever know
the pain
that awaited at the crossroads
when we had to let go?

laya

I don't think of you often,
but when I do,
my blood
goes full-tide,
a marching band
crosses my chest
in a hurry
to play for the bleeding flowers
where the land lay wounded.

I heard from someone
that you still paint faces.

do you remember mine?
seldomly,
fondly,
not at all…

I have two rose bushes now;
their thorns are your finger nails.
    under the shirt,
    beneath the sheets,
    coloured birds
    fill the planets,
    the fallen trees,
    the emerald gates.
    there was no morning then
        until morning came.

I don't know
if I ever told you…
I kept your photograph.
I pull it out sometimes
like a diving board
and look for the eastern star.

I am mistaken—
the light transfigured,
the grace removed.

in the shower,
a lone satellite
passes on the verge of night.
        I write your name upon the glass
        and gentle spheres of rain
        wash away the fingerprints.

it's a shame
this is how we were meant to go:
by water and glass,
steam and forgetting.

heartbreak

I was eleven
when it first happened...

unaware
that
there would be others,
that
there could
be *others*.

now
I laugh
in dirty
yellow rooms
wondering:
what doom
did
the early
invertebrates
feel
when they
opened their eyes
and witnessed
their first sunset?

the films are wrong

it doesn't happen
how they say…
late-night
valentine:
seeing her for the first time
wasn't slow and balmy,
dreamy and well-lit.

it was like a punch to the face
and being robbed of air,
it was like burning alive
and having the rug
ripped away beneath me.
it was a wakeup call,
a return from the dead—
and I returned
as a man
with a large void
in the shape of her.

god is a woman

I met a hurricane
last night.
she dived
right into the pool:
magazine baby,
moon
under
the water,
young red lips
spitting water at my feet.

I had film
and beer;
she was
peaches in syrup
gliding on through.

there was no rebellion from me;
I was ready for gentling.
you see,
I don't pray
and I don't think
I'll ever
come closer
than that…

on days apart

I looked for her in everything:
on the bus,
walking on the street,
in the intimate seconds
shared by strangers—
and I found her presence
in all of them.
hours spent and gone in fancy,
conjuring moments
shared between us.

I ran into a wall
the other day
and I noticed:
there is a disharmony within my being
when she is not around.
I become dysfunctionally functional—
a body
wishing it were someplace else.

people think I've gone mad…
have they forgotten what it is like?
maybe they don't know what it is like
to have someone
turning in the underbelly of the mind.

her absence filled the world
with a silent grief
and I would set fire to myself
to keep her warm again.

maybe this is madness,
but if you're not willing
to go all the way,
what's the point?

we left the garden
long ago

look
how
far
we
have
come
together

    shackle
    and
    chain breakers.

violence,
mutilation,
discordance
on the inside,
on the outside
      the running.

in our cold
and broken histories
lies a warm thread
of benevolent retaliation.

answer
Schindler,
Foley,
Kolbe,
The Chernobyl Three,
The Villagers at Eyam
and those lost names
who risked it all
so that others
may rise out of the mire.

in shadow
lies a solace
paved by the renumeration
of kindness.

and though we may do what we will
with the knowledge that binds us—
for cruelty
or for gain—
it cannot be denied.

together
we are naked
before the light,
before the dark
and the layers.
the walls,
the divides
we summon
will never
hide
this fact.

hallstatt

blue flower stuck to my leg,
white noise in my heart—
and the years run away,
and I have no intention of arriving.

after all this time,
everything in its right place
and the allegiance
I once held
drowns beneath the return
of native birds to their birthlands.

it is time;
winter is breaking.

all around,
I see paths laid out
like snakes on the cobblestone.
none
are my own;
they are tethered
to the chests
of people walking by.

those hostages of fiction
and those held up
by the normality
in the daily scene
(without sound)
they hack
and aim
and open fire at each other,
trying to keep their little worlds afloat.

I cannot save them;
I could not save you.

so, I pay them little mind
and sway
barefoot
between their crossfire.

a comfortable anarchy is mine.

today,
a curdled pig lagoon.
tomorrow,
the hermit
quite prolific in his delusions.
and I am okay
going on,
going on…

we were something worth saving
and the history books forgot about us.

swept away
above the hills,
above the salt mines
like wildfire through me—
now gone.

"goodbye!"
I howl at the ashes.

you were once
immortal,
shadow of my being.
and now
to whom shall I belong?
to the path of pleasure or peace,
it's all the same
and I must go on.

going on...

because there is something
for the underdogs—

unborn
and ahead.

can you smell it
bundled into that familiar stink?

the sand
being sand
and the sky
remembers gold
and the sun
cries orange hands.

it's all too much
to be real with yourself
or someone.

there is something terribly poetic
about not being poetic.

and places now
brave echoes and taint,
and I can't remember the faces
of the ghosts who ruined me—
only yours
like morning sun
through an ancient mist.

here
like a rogue trolley
in a parking lot,

I stand alone
on the road

hopefully lost

halfway
to hell.

Benjamin James Mclay is an Australian writer of poetry and prose and the author of *Electric Blue Heaven*. He loves horses, scotch, old trees, and his dirty little typewriter "Betty" and people who buy this book.

Printed in Australia
AUHW022219030422
361772AU00002B/2

9 780645 270204